Stella's Starliner

ROSEMARY WELLS

WALKER BOOKS
AND SUBSIDIARIES
LONDON · BOSTON · SYDNEY · AUCKLAND

Houses +
Homes

For Stella

First published 2014 by Walker Books Ltd
87 Vauxhall Walk, London SE11 5HJ

2 4 6 8 10 9 7 5 3 1

© 2014 Rosemary Wells

The right of Rosemary Wells to be identified as author/illustrator of this work has been
asserted by her in accordance with the Copyright, Designs and Patents Act 1988

This book has been typeset in Triplex Serif

Printed in China

British Library Cataloguing in Publication Data:
a catalogue record for this book is available from the British Library

ISBN 978-1-4063-5353-2

www.walker.co.uk

Stella lived in a house by the side of the road.
The house was completely silver.
It was as silver as a comet in the sky.
On its side was the word *Starliner*.

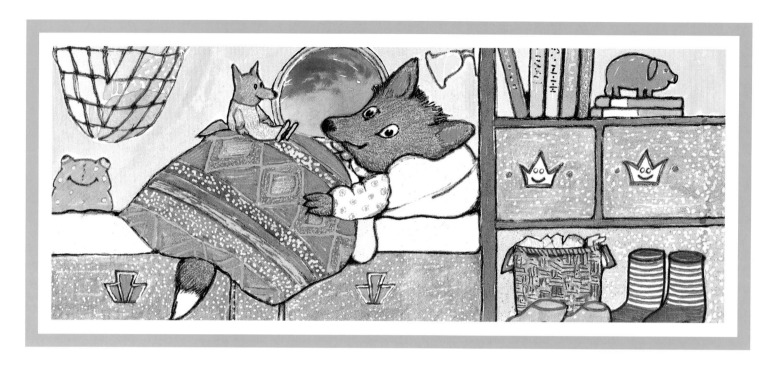

Inside was a room for sleeping and a room for being awake. There was a kitchen and a radio and a sofa that turned into a bed.

Stella had everything she needed in her silver home.

On Saturday night, Stella's daddy came home in his truck.
He parked it outside the Starliner.

On Sunday morning, Stella's mummy made pancakes for three in the tiny kitchen.

Stella's daddy took Stella fishing on Sunday afternoon.

When the sun went down, Stella's daddy kissed Stella and her mummy. He gave them all the money in his pocket. Then he started up his truck and went to work for another week. Stella and her mummy waved him all the way down to the end of the mountain road.

On Monday morning Stella and her mummy went to market.
"We'll make summer pudding," said Stella's mummy.
"And have peaches and cream!" said Stella.

Later, all the boys and girls cheered when Books on Wheels came.
Stella and her mummy read their books until they knew them
by heart. Stella didn't have a worry in the world.

Then one day a band of weasels passed by after school.
They stopped in front of the Starliner.
"Is this where you live?" the weasels asked Stella.
"Yes!" said Stella. "It's my silver home."
"Silver!" giggled one weasel. "Tin can is more like it!"
"It's an old trailer is what it is!" said another.
"You must be poor!" chimed a third.

The weasels made jokes and popped their gum all the
way down the mountain road. Their words stung Stella's
heart like the stings of bees.

At suppertime Stella could not eat.
She wanted to tell her mummy about the weasels,
but didn't want her mummy to feel the stings too.

Evening fell on the Starliner. Stella could not sleep.
Outside, the pine trees whispered in the wind.
Stella thought she heard the weasels turning cartwheels
in the night.

Late in the night, Mummy came to Stella's bedside.
"Something is wrong with my Stella," she said.
So Stella told her mummy about the stinging words.

Stella's mummy gave Stella a kiss and said,
"Look out of the window!"
Hundreds of tiny lights spun by.
"Where are we?" Stella asked.
"Sailing through the Milky Way!" said her mummy.

"Daddy has hitched our Starliner to his truck.

He's flying us far away through the night."

In the morning, the Starliner landed next to a big house.
Two bunnies came out to say hello.

One said, "I'm Grace and this is Stumpy."
"Is that your house?" asked Stumpy.
Stella didn't want to answer.

"Your house is made of silver," Stumpy went on.
"Sterling silver," added Grace. "You can tell."
"Our house is just plain old wood," said Stumpy.
"We want to see the inside!" said Grace.

Stella, Grace and Stumpy played hide-and-seek in the Starliner's secret places. They turned the sofa into a bed and the bed back into a sofa with just the touch of a button.

"You must be a millionaire to live in a silver house," said Grace.
"A zillionaire," said Stumpy.

"A squillionaire!" agreed Stella.